To: Rosemary Courtney from Jan

6   26

RABBIT MAKES A MONKEY OF LION

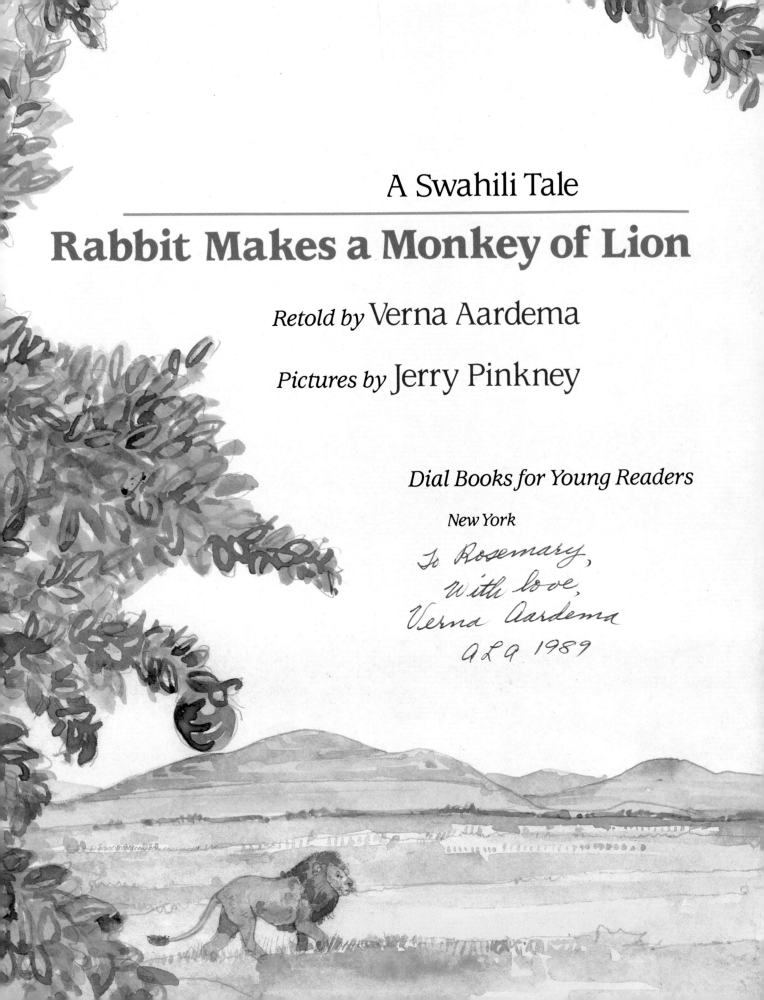

A Swahili Tale

Rabbit Makes a Monkey of Lion

Retold by Verna Aardema

Pictures by Jerry Pinkney

Dial Books for Young Readers

New York

To Rosemary,
With love,
Verna Aardema
ALA 1989

For little Ian Adsit,
who made a great-grandmother of me

V.A.

To Ben Black, friend and mentor

J.P.

Published by Dial Books for Young Readers
A Division of NAL Penguin Inc.
2 Park Avenue
New York, New York 10016

Published simultaneously in Canada by
Fitzhenry & Whiteside Limited, Toronto
Printed in Hong Kong by South China Printing Co.
First Edition
(b)
1 2 3 4 5 6 7 8 9 10

Rabbit Makes a Monkey of Lion is retold from "The Hare
and the Lion" in *Zanzibar Tales,* by George W. Bateman,
published by A. C. McClurg and Co., Chicago, 1901.

Library of Congress Cataloging in Publication Data

Aardema, Verna / Rabbit makes a monkey of Lion.

Summary: With the help of her friends Bush-rat
and Turtle, smart and nimble Rabbit makes a fool
of the mighty but slow-witted king of the forest.
[1. Folklore—Africa. 2. Animals—Folklore.]
I. Pinkney, Jerry, ill. II. Title.
PZ8.1.A213Rab 1989   398.2'452'096 [E]   86-11523
ISBN 0-8037-0297-3 / ISBN 0-8037-0298-1 (lib. bdg.)

The full-color artwork was prepared using pencil, colored
pencils, and watercolor. It was then color-separated
and reproduced as red, blue, yellow, and black halftones.

There was a time when, of all creatures in the world, monkey was considered most foolish. So whenever an animal was tricked by someone, he would cry, "That rascal made a monkey of me!"

In this tale about making a monkey of Lion, the honey guide starts it all.

One morning Rabbit was wakened by a honey guide singing outside her door:

Chee, chee! Come and see—
A bees' nest in a calabash tree.

Rabbit followed the little bird as she flitted ahead and led her to a calabash tree. There high up in the trunk of it was a bees' nest. Rabbit thanked the bird.

Then she went to Bush-rat and said, "I know where there's a bee tree. Come and help me get honey."

Bush-rat smacked his lips, *pih, pih, pih.* He said, "Legs rest, but the mouth does not. Take me to that honey."

The two gathered some dry banana leaves and climbed the calabash tree. They lit one of the leaves and smoked out the bees. Then they began eating the honey, *fweo, fweo, fweo.*

Suddenly, HUNNN! There was a lion below them. He growled, "Who's up there eating my honey?"

"It's only us," squeaked the bush-rat.

"Aha!" cried Lion. "I know your voice, Bush-rat."

Rabbit whispered, "Hush, Bush-rat! Wrap me in these leftover leaves and drop me down. We will fool that lion!"

So the bush-rat wrapped the rabbit in the long banana leaves and dropped her. The bundle fell, KATOM!

Lion said, "Hmm. What's that?" Then he saw the rabbit wriggle out and go running, *yiridi, yiridi, yiridi,* into the forest.

Lion tore after her. But the rabbit managed to keep a jump ahead of him, and finally dove into some brambles.

Lion scrambled, *zak, vak, dilak,* around the thorny thicket. But he could not find an opening. "That little rascal made a monkey of me!" he cried.

When Lion went back to catch the bush-rat, he was gone too! He looked for him and found him digging yams in his garden.

Bush-rat saw Lion coming. He called, "Oh, Lion, I'm getting these yams to pay you for the honey."

"Hmm," said Lion. "Yams won't do. I'm going to eat YOU!"

"Oh, please eat this fine yam first," begged Bush-rat. "Here, catch it!" He tossed a yam high.

Lion threw his head back and opened his mouth wide.

And Bush-rat went RAS toward a hole under the roots of a nearby tree.

The lion caught the yam. But when he looked for the bush-rat, all he saw was his tail disappearing into the burrow.

Lion tried frantically to dig him out. The sand flew, *freh, freh, freh, freh!* But the burrow was too deep. "That little rascal made a monkey of me!" he cried.

The next morning Rabbit was wakened again by the honey guide singing:

Chee, chee! Come and see—
A bees' nest in a calabash tree.

Rabbit knew that she should not go back to that bee tree. Still, she remembered how sweet the honey was. And at last she followed the bird to the calabash tree.

She went to Turtle and said, "I know where there's a bee tree. Come and help me get honey."

"Umm!" cried the turtle as she rubbed her belly. "When you say *honey,* I can hear you with one ear. Take me to that bee tree."

The two gathered some leaves and climbed the calabash tree. They smoked out the bees and ate honey until they felt sick. Then they picked a big calabash and dug out the seeds, intending to fill it with honeycomb dripping with honey.

Suddenly, HUNNN! There was the lion below them. He growled, "Who's up there stealing my honey?"

"It's only us," said Turtle.

"Hush," whispered Rabbit as she climbed into the calabash. "Put the top on and drop me down. We will fool that lion!"

So Turtle put the stem end back on the gourd, and called, "Stand back, Lion. Here comes a calabash."

Now, that calabash had not had time to dry and harden. So when it whirled to the ground, it smashed into bits, NGISH! And there was the slightly stunned rabbit lying in the middle.

Lion pounced upon her, TWOM! "At last I have you," he roared. "And I'm going to eat you!"

Rabbit woke up in a hurry. She cried, "But I'm too tough to eat. You have to make me tender first."

"How?" snarled the lion.

Rabbit said, "Take me by the tail and twirl me round and round."
But the tail of a rabbit is little more than a ball of fuzz. And when
Lion grasped Rabbit's tail and twirled her, she went flying—WEO—
into the forest. All Lion had left in his claws were a few brown hairs.
He said, "That little rascal made a monkey of me again!"

This time the lion did not chase the rabbit. He waited for the other thief to come down from the tree.

When Turtle reached the ground, she drew her head and tail and feet into her shell. Lion tapped the top shell, *tak, tak, tak.* He turned the turtle over and tapped the bottom shell, *tuk, tuk, tuk.* "How can I make a meal of this?" he grumbled.

"It's easy," cried Turtle from inside her shell. "First you must take me to a water hole."

So Lion carried the turtle to a small pond.

"Now," said Turtle, "put me into the muddy water and pile mud on top of me. When I'm covered well, scrub me hard and my shell will come off."

Lion put the turtle into the murky water at the edge of the pond. And he scooped mud on top of her, *kahta-KUM, kahta-KUM, kahta-KUM.* "Is that enough?" he asked.

"Can you see me?" asked Turtle.

Lion looked on this side. He looked on that side. "A little bit," he said.

"It's not enough," said Turtle.

Then, as the lion piled on more mud, the turtle slipped away under the water, *pesi, pesi, pesi.* Lion did not realize what was happening until he saw the laughing face of the turtle pop up in the middle of the pond. He hurled a lump of mud at her, ZEEE! "That little rascal made a monkey of me!" he cried.

As he walked away, Lion began thinking about his troubles. First it was Rabbit and Bush-rat making a fool of him. Then it was Rabbit and Turtle. Aha! Rabbit was behind it all!

Lion's mane bristled, HIRRR! He set out for Rabbit's house, saying, "I'll gobble her up!" But when he arrived, she was not at home. He went inside and waited for her to come.

At dusk Rabbit returned. As she approached her house, she saw lion tracks near the door. She went back a little way. If the lion was in her house, she would have to get him out!

Rabbit knew just what to do. "How-de-do, Little House!" she called.

No answer.

Rabbit called again, "Little House, you always tell me *how-de-do*. Is something wrong today?"

No answer.

Rabbit tried again, "Little House, ANSWER me!"

This confused the lion. Finally, trying to talk like a house, he answered, "How-de-do."

Rabbit laughed, *kye, kye, kye!* "You foolish lion!" she cried. "Don't you know that a house can't talk?"

Then, HARRR! Lion burst out of the house and went roaring after the rabbit.

Rabbit ran for her life, zigzagging between the trees and—just in time—finding safety in a thicket.

Lion turned away, saying, "That little rascal made a monkey of me again!" As he set out for home, he shook his shaggy head and said, "Rabbits are just too hard to catch."